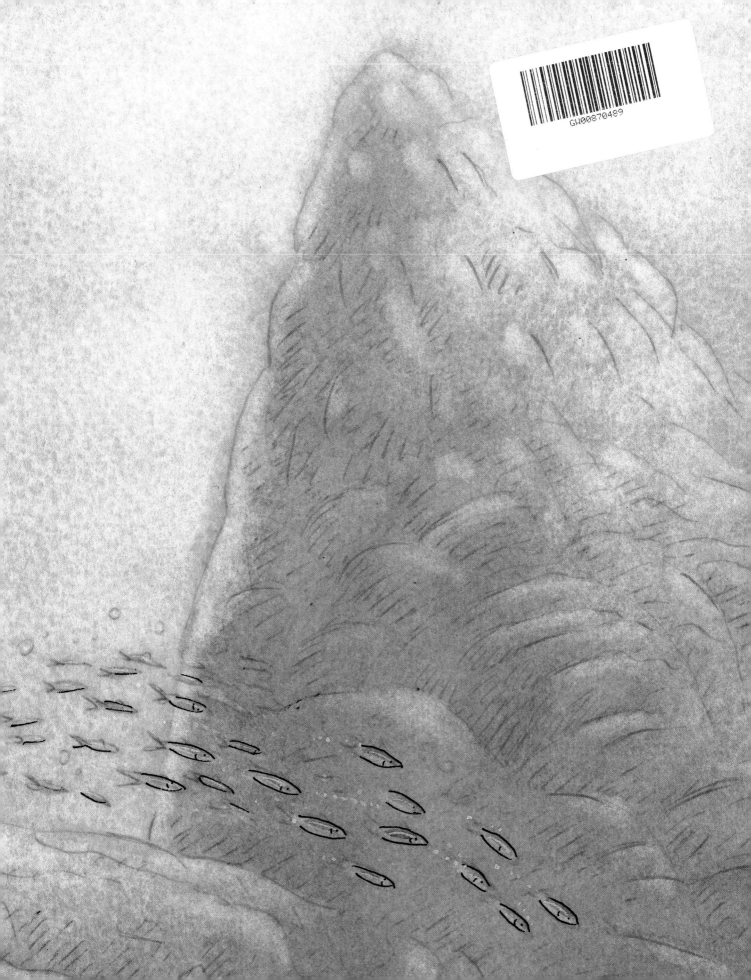

For Elma, with love
G.W.

For Hannah, with love
C.S.

First published 1990 by
Walker Books Ltd, 87 Vauxhall Walk, London SE11 5HJ

Text © 1990 Gina Wilson. Illustrations © 1990 Clive Scruton

First printed 1990. Printed in Hong Kong by Imago

British Library Cataloguing in Publication Data
Wilson, Gina. Wompus Galumpus.   I.Title   II.Scruton, Clive.   823'.914[J]

ISBN 0-7445-1142-9

WOMPUS GALUMPUS

KING·OF·THE·DEEP

Written by Gina Wilson   Illustrated by Clive Scruton

WALKER BOOKS
LONDON

Wompus Galumpus lived in a cave at the bottom of the sea. He called himself "King of the Deep", but he wasn't really king of anything. He just liked the idea. He was big, and slippery all over, like jelly. He could flop himself down, or stretch out thin or draw himself bolt upright.

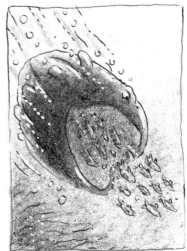

Sometimes he made himself rocket-shaped and zoomed around, frightening pretty little starfish. Other times he spent the day looking pretty himself, tingle-tangling on the tide like a jellyfish.

He could eat *anything* – seaweed and pebbles, mussels and limpets, stingrays and eels, and even bottles and old tin cans flung overboard from passing ships. "I'm not a fusspot!" he would remark, gulping down shoals of haddock. "Anything goes!"

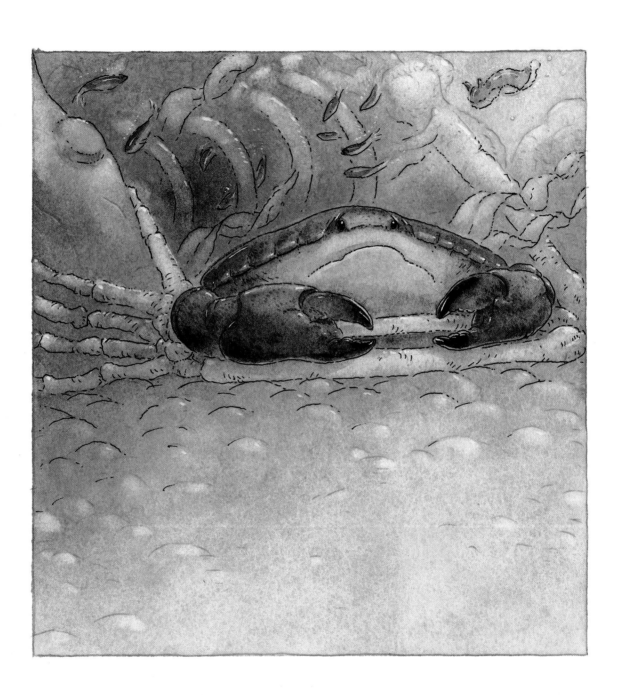

Across the mouth of Wompus's cave lay the skeleton of a
drunken sailor, bottle in hand. This was the home of a giant crab
called Crustus. Crustus crouched among the wave-whitened
bones, keeping watch with his pin-point eyes.

Crustus and Wompus were friends, except when Wompus was
in an eating mood. Then Crustus would close his eyes, pull in
his legs and cower under his carapace.

"Cock-eyed crustacean!" Wompus would snort between
mouthfuls. "As if I would eat a friend!"

On calm evenings they chatted together as the sun went down
and, one by one, like stars, the luminous
little tiddlers came out.

One morning Wompus awoke from a sleep that had lasted a week. He sploshed to the front of his cave and gave himself a stretch.

"A-a-ark!" warned Crustus, flickering an eye upwards.

"Blistering barracuda!" foamed Wompus. "Intruders!"

"Monster-hunters, maybe!" quavered the crab. "If they get so much as a whiff they'll be down here with nets!"

"*Nets*!" scoffed Wompus. "Use your cranium, crab! What's a net against a Wompus?" All the same, he flopped down like a ton of tar to think about it.

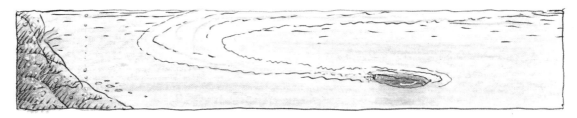

Overhead, the boat started up with a deafening boom and chugged away. Crustus felt happy again. He scuttled round collecting food for his lunch.

"That's *it*!" exclaimed Wompus suddenly.

Crustus jumped.

"If they can do it, so can we," said Wompus. "Let's go exploring!"

"Where to?"

"Rockpools. You can be my guide."

"You'll never fit in a rockpool!"

"Crackpate! I shan't stop there. I shall go on."

"Will you really?" quivered the crab. "I think rockpools might be far enough for me."

"In that case," said Wompus, "I shall have to go on alone." He towered up tall. "I'm Wompus Galumpus. I'm not afraid."

They set off that night, Crustus leading the way. Wompus frolicked above him. "I'm Wompus Galumpus!" he sang as he went. "Follow me!"

And behind them came crayfish and monkfish, and mackerel and mullet, and dolphins and whiting and red-spotted plaice, and dogfish and catfish and fish no one has ever put a name to – all shimmering their scales and popping out bubbles like balloons.

By dawn they reached shallow waters. Wompus spread himself, paper-thin, over the surface.

"You look like an oil slick!" cackled Crustus.

"I come in peace," whispered Wompus, turning thinner than ever. His voice was like the sift of a sea breeze.

"Metamorphic mollusc! What a brilliant disguise!" exclaimed Crustus. As they allowed themselves to be gently *shoofed* up on

the strand, he scuttled away to a deep cleft between nearby rocks.

"If they catch me, they'll boil me pink as a pig!" he quavered.
"You're all right. No one would know
what to do with you!"

But Wompus was snuffling like a
newborn baby. "I'm drowning,"
he panted, "in *air*!"

Crustus emerged from the cleft at once. "Let's go back!"

"Just ... a ... minute..." Wompus was getting the hang of it. His breaths were coming in short puffs, and then in sighs, and, at last, in smooth, sweet streams. "Ah!" he grinned. "That's it!" Then, right before Crustus's bobbling eyes, he rolled himself up tight and bounced away.

"Suffering swordfish!" thought Crustus. "How's he going to disguise his *smell?*" Deep down in the sea, Wompus had a very fine fishy smell indeed, but up here you could say it was a *stink*. The smell of him hung in the air like a drizzle of cod-liver

oil. "*I* like it," thought Crustus, breathing in deeply, "but no one else will!"

Wompus couldn't actually smell himself. Leaving Crustus behind, he bounced gleefully over the sands. He bounced up steep steps to the cliff top and rolled to the edge. The beach spread out before him and, far away now, he could just see the whispering, outgoing sea. For a second he felt a wild surge of longing. Oh, to be plunging ... and spouting ... and spurting! Wait for me! Wait for me! But he turned inland again, bravely. This was why he had come.

He rolled along the gritty, cliff-top road. It was making him sore. He wished he could fly, like the beaky gannet screeching overhead.

The sun rose higher and hotter. He dropped into a shady, damp gutter and sighed. Ahead was the main street of Swillock-on-Sea. He rolled slowly forward.

Houses rose tall on either side. A shiny square in one of the walls opened up suddenly and a human face popped out. It puckered. "Pooh! Ugh!" The window closed again with a bang!

"Flippin' fins! They don't like my smell!" thought Wompus. He rolled quickly round a corner, and then round another.

Now, a large hairy dog was sniffing, short-sightedly, towards him. In a flash Wompus stretched himself out, flat and treacly. The dog snuffled up till its nose bumped into him. Then it jerked back its head, shook the hair out of its eyes, and gave an excited little yelp. How niffy and licksome! It dropped out its pink, ribbony tongue and slapped it back and forth over Wompus like a paintbrush.

Wompus tingled with pleasure. He was wet all over! What a wonderful welcome! As the dog went on its way, he pulled himself together again and flopped happily along in splodgy hops.

All at once, a grim, rumbling roar filled the air. Wompus waited, rooted to the spot with fright. Then suddenly a ramshackle truck full of workmen, and picks, and shovels, came rattling round the corner and jolted to a halt. Wompus splatted himself flat in the road again and watched through one eye. The men peered forward. A boy jumped from the back of the truck and advanced on him. "You moved!" he said, nudging Wompus with a mucky boot. Wompus closed his eye.

The truck started up again and rolled slowly towards them. "Stop messing!" shouted the driver. His face was screwed up. He was trying not to breathe.

"It moved!" shrilled the boy. "Din' you see? It was six foot tall when we came roun' the corner – wi' tons of little arms. It's a monster from outer space!"

The man laughed. "Jump in before we're all gassed out!" He inched the truck up to Wompus, then calmly drove it straight over him, leaving deep tyre tracks across his silky surface.

Wompus throbbed as the truck disappeared. As its roar died away, he squirmed himself into a bruised huddle. "That's *it*!" thought Wompus. "The sea for me!"

Too late! The bell inside a pointy tower nearby chimed eight and suddenly the street filled with people scurrying to work.

"E-e-e-eugh!" they gasped, peering down at Wompus and turning green. "What a stench! What a stink! What a pong! What *is* it?"

"It'll dry up if we leave it alone," said a woman with a stiff broom. "It'll shrink. It'll shrivel clean away, whatever it is. Look, it's curling at the edges, already!" She scratched her broom back and forth over Wompus. It felt like sandpaper.

"It's flaking like old paint," said someone else. "That's right, Mrs Sprockett, you take your brush to it."

"Today's going to be a scorcher," said yet another. "It said on the weather. The hottest since records began."

The woman with the brush gave Wompus a final poke. "You would have to park yourself outside *my* shop," she muttered. "Who's going to buy fish-scented flowers?"

Wompus sweltered. His skin grew tight and prickly. Buses showered him with gravel. Schoolboys trampled over him to see the marks left by the soles of their shoes.

The sun beat down.

By nine o'clock the street was still again. By ten … and eleven
… silence had fallen over the whole of Swillock-on-Sea.

Wompus opened a lacklustre eye. Heat shimmered from the
road. Blinds were drawn over windows. Nothing stirred.

Little by little, he pulled himself together. At least he *tried* to.
He tugged and tugged. He heaved and hauled. He yanked and
jerked. But nothing happened!

"I'm sizzling away!" he wheezed in panic. "*Help*!" he roared in his loudest voice. But it sounded like the air leaking out of a bicycle tyre.

Mrs Sprockett came out from her flower shop. "Drying up nicely, you nasty blot!" She sniffed. "Smell's not so bad now either!"

Wompus was *stuck*. His skin was all dull. It was blistering and puckering. Bit by bit, he could feel himself evaporating.

At lunch-time a little girl came skipping along the pavement. She was carrying a fifty pence piece to buy daisies from Mrs Sprockett. All of a sudden, she tripped and fell, right beside Wompus. The fifty pence piece shot from her hand and landed plumb on his middle. It twinkled there on his wrinkly old skin.

The little girl sat on the edge of the pavement, dabbing at her bleeding knee. She sobbed, and her bright, round tears splashed down on Wompus – the sweetest brine he had ever tasted! Wompus gave the little girl a wink. He twitched his leathery skin till the fifty pence piece ended up beside her little bare feet.

She stared in amazement. Wompus sighed. He winked again and the little girl laughed like the tinkling of shells on a coral reef.

Mrs Sprockett came out with her broom. "Get your feet out of that filth, Martha Louise!"

"It winked," said Martha Louise. "It wants a drink. It's alive."

"What a horrible idea," shuddered Mrs Sprockett. She filled Martha Louise's arms with daisies and hurried away to her till with the fifty pence piece.

"You *do* want a drink, don't you?" whispered Martha Louise, bending low over Wompus. She reached out and overturned one of Mrs Sprockett's buckets. Water splooshed down into the gutter. It was stale and green and full of daisy stalks. But to Wompus it tasted like champagne!

"Thank you, Martha Louise," he whispered. But the little girl was sprinting away.

Mrs Sprockett puffed and panted at the edge of the kerb. She shook her fist at Wompus. "I'll give you winking!" she hissed. "I'll give you wanting a drink! If you're still here at the end of the day, I'll burn you up with the rest of my rubbish!"

"O-o-o-oh!" Wompus shrank deeper into the gutter, trying to suck up every drop of moisture. If only Martha Louise had doused him with all the buckets. Overhead, the sun throbbed. "O-o-o-oh, Crustus!" he whimpered.

Down by the water's edge, Crustus had spent the day hidden in the rocks. Through a crevice, he had watched the sun burning on sand and sea. He had dozed, his head muzzy with the strong, thick scent of Wompus Galumpus.

The day advanced, and that wonderful scent grew weaker and weaker. A tremor of worry stirred under Crustus's corny, hard shell.

It was *hot*, so hot that by lunch-time the squealing crowds packed up their deck chairs and buckets and spades and left the sands to find shelter inland. Then Crustus realized that the scent of Wompus had faded ... completely ... *away*!

He clambered stiffly out of his hiding place. He scuttled, all sideways, across the sands, following the trail of Wompus's early-morning bouncing. On the sands he felt safe, almost invisible. But, up on the esplanade, he felt very *un*safe. A giant crab could be supper for six people, or seven, or eight – if you could find a pot big enough.

He darted along behind billboards and dustbins. He ducked
out of sight in gutters. By fits and starts, *almost* losing the scent,
he followed where Wompus had been. And at five o'clock, on
the dot, he turned into the street where Wompus still *was*!

Mrs Sprockett was out on the pavement, inspecting the blot on
her landscape. "Well, well," she said, rubbing her hands.
"Nothing much left of you, now. I'll dig a little hole in my garden
and bury you. That's what I'll do. If I burn you, you'll only turn
smelly again – like an old rubber tyre."

Crustus crept forward. The pavements were jostling with
people coming home from their work. They turned their faces
up to catch the gentle rays of evening sun. They didn't see the
crab at their feet. But Crustus had spotted a splodge – a chewy,
black lump of a thing. He hurtled towards it. He prodded it with
a claw. "Wompus! Wompus! Is that you?"

Wompus was too feeble to reply. But just the ghost of the old smell was there. Crustus set to work with his corny pincers. As gently as he could, he peeled his friend from the cruel concrete. He flipped him up in the air, and caught him, *pflaff*, on his back! Then they were off – clattering and galloping, eight legs at once, down the middle of the main street of Swillock-on-Sea.

People gawped. Then they came to their senses and chased along behind. Martha Louise led the way, clapping and cheering. Then came Mrs Sprockett, waving a spade. Traffic skidded and hooted. People of all shapes and sizes rushed out into the street and joined the stampede.

Crustus thundered to the top of the steps. He careered down
them, four at a time. He raced over the golden sands to
the murmuring sea. "You've won!" whooped Martha
Louise as he tumbled into the rippling wavelets and
tossed Wompus back into his kingdom at last!

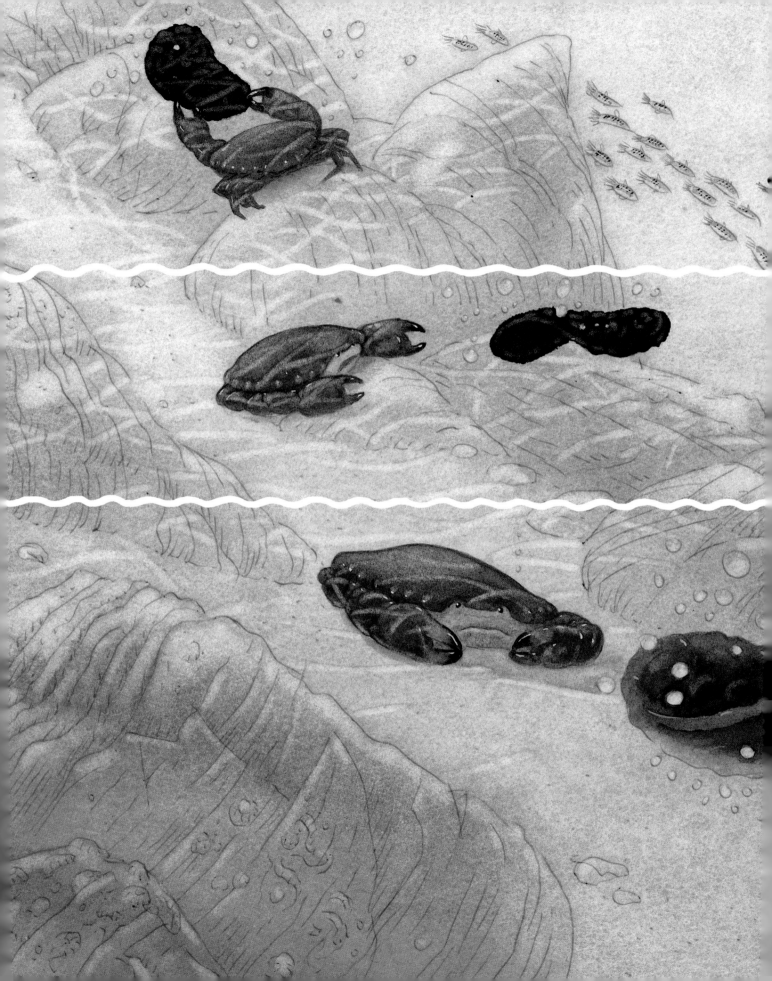

Wompus drifted in the shallows, limp and lifeless. Crustus stared in dismay. "Come on! We're going home!" With one last burst of strength he gripped Wompus between his pincers and dragged him out to sea. Deeper and deeper they went. And just as Crustus was giving up hope, and great crabby tears were squeezing from his eyes and adding themselves to the wondrous volume of the ocean, Wompus *moved*!

Crustus opened his claws. Wompus floated free and sailed dreamily along beside him. Then he gave a little shiver and a shake … and his edges were growing silky again…

"What's this?" said a nosy old sprat, swimming alongside.

Wompus gulped. He stretched. Like a magician's silk scarf, he grew and he grew till he waved through the deep like the banner of a conquering hero.

"*We* know who you are!" bubbled crayfish and monkfish, and mackerel and mullet, and dolphins and whiting and red-spotted plaice, and dogfish and catfish and fish no one has ever put a name to.

"Oh, my!" said the sprat. "You're Wompus Galumpus, the King of the…"

"DEEP!" roared Wompus. "Yes, that's who I am. Follow me!"

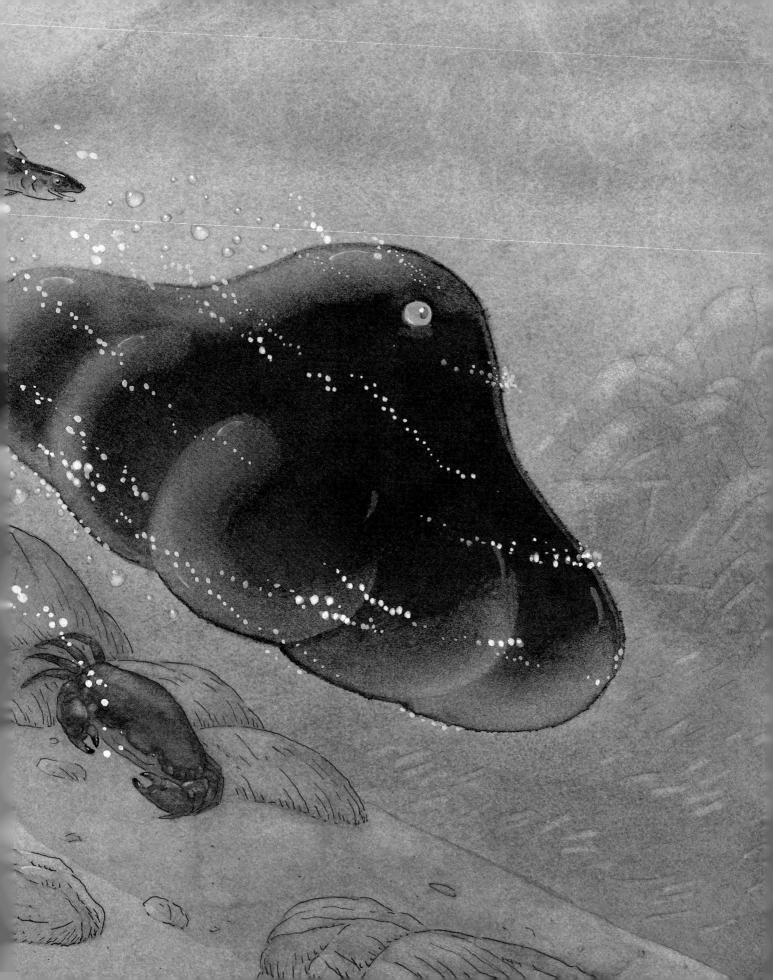

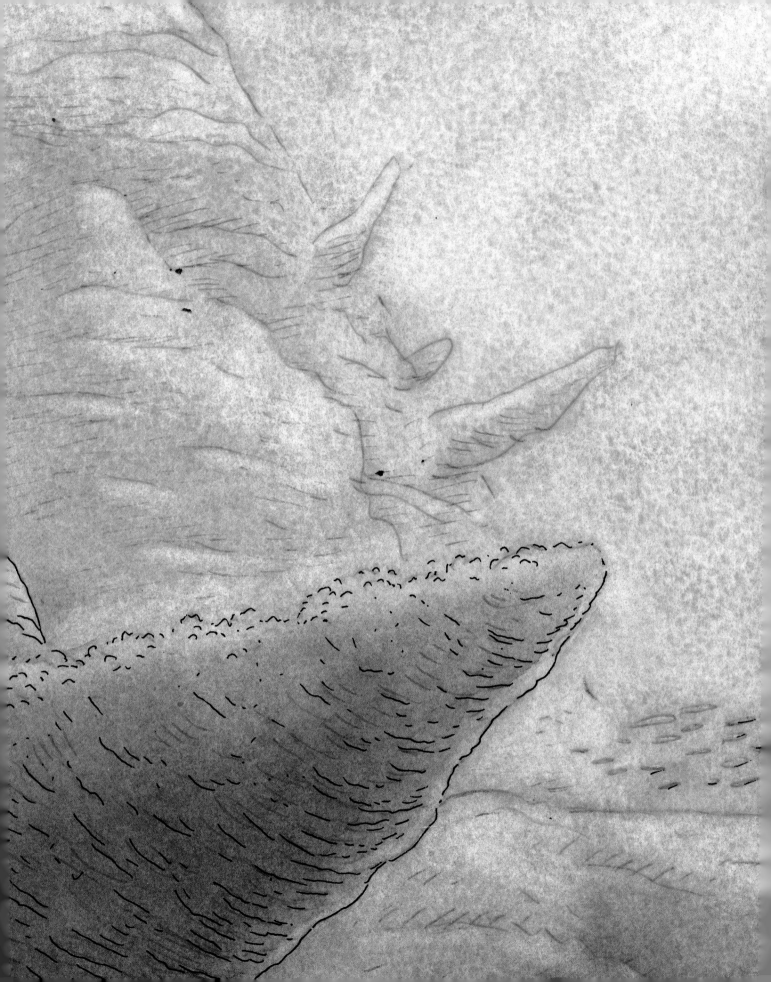